By Meredith Rusu

ISBN 978-1-338-10882-8

10 9 8 7 6 5 4 3 2 1 17 18 19 20 21

Printed in the U.S.A. 132

First printing 2017

Book design by Erin McMahon

SCHOLASTIC INC.

It is a very special day in Shopville. All of the Shopkins are gathered in Small Mart for a sweet treat. What could have everyone bubbling with excitement?

"Happy Easter, Shopkins! And welcome to this year's Great Chocolate Hunt!" says Apple Blossom.

"Hooray!" everyone cheers. The Great Chocolate Hunt is Shopville's biggest Easter tradition.
shop...You can't stop!

Apple explains the rules. "Cheeky Chocolate will hide somewhere in the store. The first Shopkin to find her wins a fabulous prize."

"This year's prizes are . . . a new car!"

"Yay!" cheer the Shopkins.

"Or a new . . . ish Easter bunny!" says Apple.

"But if we don't find Cheeky, then she gets a prize," says Apple.

Cheeky grins. "I've totally got this in the bag. I'm going to look like one hot chocolate riding in my new car!"

"On your mark . . . get set . . . GO!" shouts Apple.

Everyone races after Cheeky! Everyone except Kooky Cookie.

"Kooky, aren't you going to look for Cheeky?" asks Apple.

"Uh-huh," says Kooky.

"Aren't you going to run?" asks Apple.

"Nuh-uh," says Kooky.

Meanwhile, Strawberry Kiss and Lippy Lips have a plan.
"If we search together, there's no way Cheeky can hide from us!" gushes Strawberry.
"Right!" says Lippy. "By the way . . . have you seen Shady Diva's new *Glazed Donut* fashion collection? Isn't it just the sweetest?"

Strawberry and Lippy are too busy chatting to notice Cheeky sneaking away.
Maybe they should have spent more time looking and less time gabbing.

Meanwhile, Slick Breadstick is hot on Cheeky's trail.

"Come here, my darling," he calls. "You cannot get away. Nothing will distract me!"

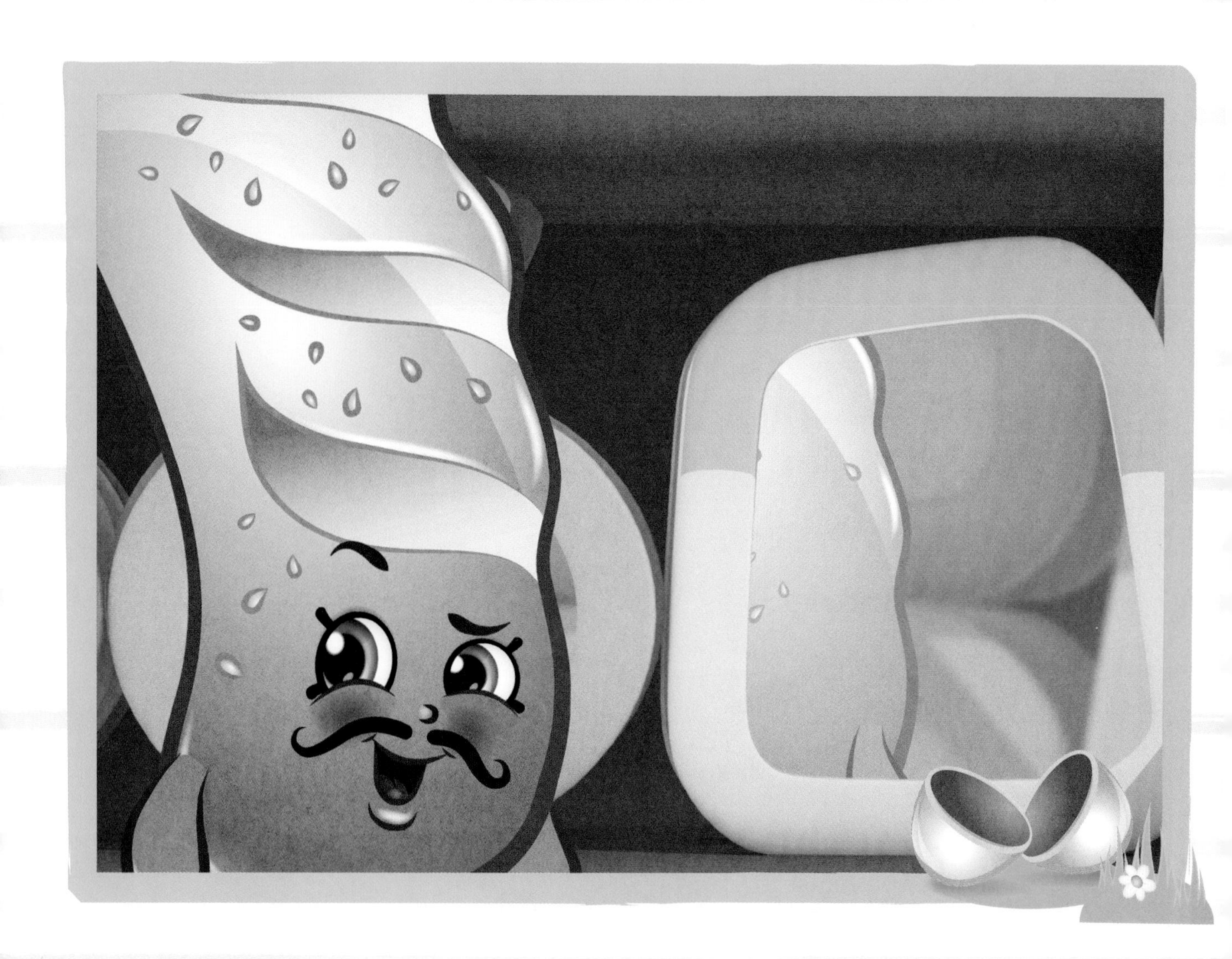

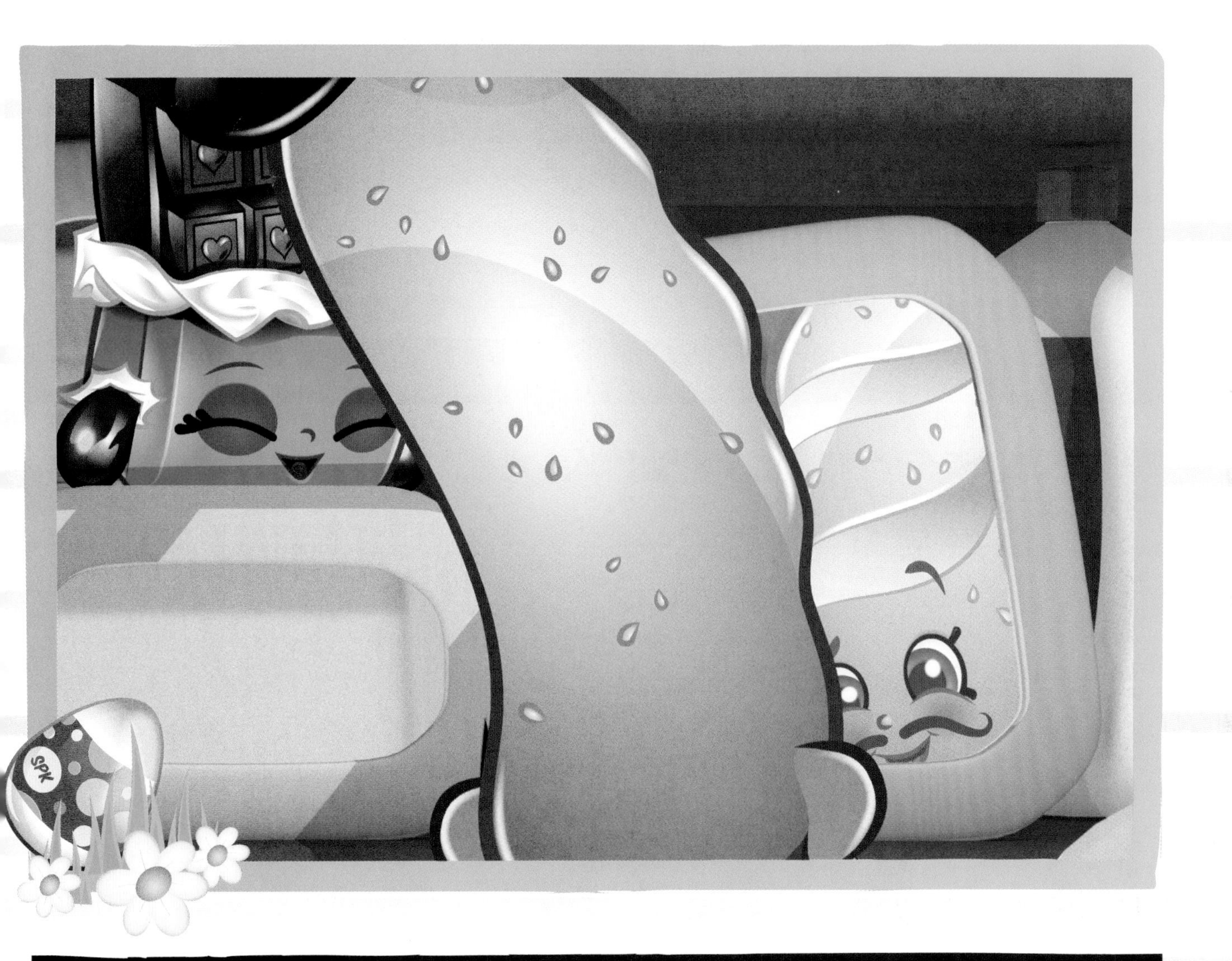

Suddenly, Slick stops as he walks by a mirror.

"I forgot just how fresh-baked and handsome I am!" he exclaims. He is so distracted by his reflection that he doesn't see Cheeky hiding nearby.

Cheeky has escaped again!

Cheeky sneaks up to the Small Mart announcement booth.

"Heh, heh, heh," she chuckles. "No one will think to look for me here."

But Cheeky looks down and sees someone coming closer.

"Oh, crumbs—it's Apple Blossom!" Cheeky says to herself. "I need to distract her before my chances of winning melt away!"

Cheeky thinks fast. She makes an announcement over the Small Mart loudspeaker.

"It sure is stinky in this aisle. No one will ever come looking here!"

Apple hears the announcement. She gasps. Did Cheeky just give away her hiding spot in the cheese aisle?

The other Shopkins hear it, too.
Everyone races to the cheese aisle!

Apple, Lippy, Strawberry, and Slick get to the cheese aisle. But Cheeky is nowhere to be found.
"I do not understand," says Slick. "Cheeky said she was in ze stinky aisle, no?"

"Isn't it obvious?" says Lippy. "We've been tricked!"

"Oh, this is the berry worst!" wails Strawberry. "Cheeky is going to win!"

Up in the booth, Cheeky is very pleased with herself. "My plan was baked to perfection," she says. "Now I'll go to my real secret hiding spot. That car is as good as mine. This is the best Easter ever!"

Back in the cheese aisle, Apple shrugs. "It looks like we've been outsmarted. I officially declare Cheeky as the win—"

"AHHHHHH!" a voice suddenly cries out.

The Shopkins gasp. That sounds like Cheeky!

Everyone races back to the starting line. Cheeky has been captured by . . . Kooky?!

"Cheeky! Are you okay?" asks Apple.

"Yes," groans Cheeky. "Just get Kooky off me."

"What happened?" asks Apple.

"Well, I didn't think anyone would be silly enough to stay at the starting line," explains Cheeky. "But when I got here, Kooky jumped on me. I never stood a chance."

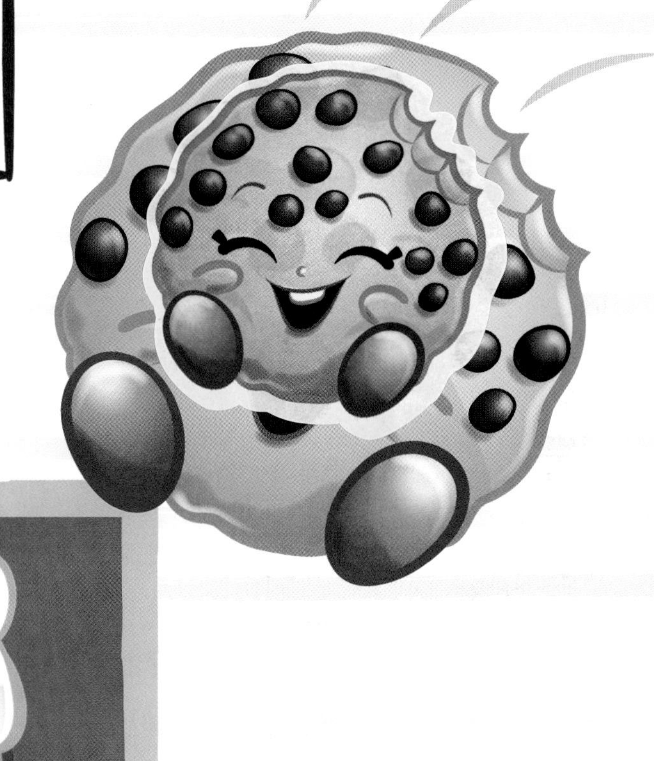

"Congratulations, Kooky!" says Apple. "You're this year's Great Chocolate Hunt winner! Pick whichever prize you like."

Everyone is sure that Kooky will pick the shiny new car.

"Ugh," groans Cheeky. "Can I at least borrow the car, Kooky?"

But Kooky does not pick the car.

She picks the Easter bunny!

"How can you pick that bunny over a cool new car?" cries Cheeky.

"*Ahhhhhhh,*" says Kooky happily, snuggling her new bunny friend.

Oh, well. It looks like it's been a positively kooky ending to the Great Chocolate Hunt.

Until next Easter . . . check ya later!